CreativeKids
p u b l i s h i n g

ISBN 978-1-55454-451-6

Copyright © 2008 Creative Kids Publishing, a division of
Transglobal Communications Group, Inc.
5550 Skylane Boulevard, Suite G
Santa Rosa, CA 95403

No part of this publication may be reproduced, stored in a
retrieval system or transmitted in any form by any means,
electronic, mechanical, photocopying, recording or otherwise,
without prior written permission of the publisher.

All rights reserved.

Written and Illustrated by:

Mike Boldt

"Looks like clear skies tonight sir," Blitz reported as he checked his instruments.

"Fantastic! I still remember that blizzard we had to fly through last year," said Santa Bearclaws. "It looks as though this Christmas Eve will be smooth sailing."

BOOM! Suddenly a cannon ball shot straight through the side of the sleigh.

Blitz and Donna did their best to fly the smoking wreck, but the sleigh spiraled down and crashed with an enormous splash in the middle of North Pole Forest Lake.

"Is everyone okay?" Santa Bearclaws quickly asked as soon as he had recovered.

"All fine sir," came the response from the group.

They all sat there a little wet and cold and confused, then slowly out of the mist, a huge ship appeared.

"We're saved!" the elves cheered. "Hello! Hello! We are over here!"

But their excitement was quieted by a song that floated down to their ears.

"Yo-ho-ho, Yo-ho-hum! We be Present Pirates and here we come!"

Within the blink of an eye, Santa, Leonard, Donna, Blitz, and a couple of elves were aboard the ship and tied up as prisoners! They could do nothing but watch as the singing and dancing pirates hauled all the presents on deck.

There was a shout that stopped all the commotion and one large pirate stepped forward with a large smile, "I be Cap'n Silvertoof, arrr, and these be me crew!"

"We be called ye Present Pirates. Welcome aboard me ship, the *Nauttylist.*"

Santa and the North Pole gang sat stunned as Silvertoof continued. "Since pirates we be, we don't get presents see. So we sail the seas in search of present treasure and indeed we have captured a mighty booty tonight!"

"But those presents are for all the kids who now won't get any because you stole them," said Santa. "You are only on the *Naughty List* because you steal."

"What arrrr ye saying, landlubber?" Silvertoof asked.

"Well," Santa said. "You would all get presents if you didn't steal anymore!"

"Well shiver me timbers!" Silvertoof exclaimed. "This be most terrible news that we have ruined Christmas. Arrrr, we shall surely be on the *Naughty List* forever!"

"Well maybe you could help us still," Santa said encouragingly. "After all, the night is still young."

"The sleigh has a hole in it though sir, and can't fly," Leonard pointed out.

"Ahoy! But me thinks her engines be fine!" Silvertoof said. "This ol' seadog has a few tricks up his sleeve yet."

"All right step lightly maties, batten down the hatches, and man the riggings. I wanna see that sleigh atop the mast lickety split."

As Captain Silvertoof continued to bark orders at the crew members, Santa could only watch in amazement, as Silvertoof's fantastic plan took shape right before him.

"Arrrr! Raise the anchor! Time to set off," came Silvertoof's last order.

Blitz fired up the engines, and slowly and almost magically; the sleigh, the crew, and even the entire ship took off into the Christmas Eve sky. Everyone let out cheers; well—except for Leonard, who was stuck on the mast and couldn't get down!

As they sailed through the night, all you could hear was a joyous chorus of "Yo Ho Ho Ho, Merry Christmas!"